22139482

LETTERS I

This book is to be returned on or before
the last date stamped below.

1.		5.
2.		6.
3.		7.
4.		8.

LETTERS FROM A MOUSE

To The Maggott
and all my other cats
H.B.

First published 1997 by Walker Books Ltd
87 Vauxhall Walk, London SE11 5HJ

This edition published 1997

4 6 8 10 9 7 5 3

Text © 1997 Herbie Brennan
Illustrations © 1997 Louise Voce

This book has been typeset in Courier.

Printed in Great Britain by Clays Ltd, St Ives plc

British Library Cataloguing in Publication Data
A catalogue record for this book is
available from the British Library.

ISBN 0-7445-4761-X

LETTERS FROM A MOUSE

HERBIE BRENNAN

Illustrations by
LOUISE VOCE

WALKER BOOKS
AND SUBSIDIARIES

LONDON • BOSTON • SYDNEY

hayes bros. ltd. OFFICE SUPPLIES

8 Grafton Street, London W1X 3LA England Tel: 0171 123 4789 Fax: 031 4933061

Directors: J. Hayes H. Hayes

dear customer,

i am s. mouse of hayes bros. ltd. and im the boss.
when harry hayes and joe hayes go home for the
night, im in charge.

i can sit on joes swivel chair.
i can put my feet up on harrys desk.

i can sniff around inside the filing cabinet.
i can do anything i want.

but now im in trouble for answering the phone.

last night a man rang up and said, please send me
- a box of carbon paper
- a ream of typing paper, bond
- a ribbon for an ibm electric
- a brief case big enough to hold half a million
  pounds in unmarked 5 pound notes
- a printer stand
- two typing chairs and
- a palatino golf ball.

we dont do sporting goods, i said.
the golf balls for my ibm electric, he said. all
right, i said. all right what, he said. all right
i can send out your order, i said.
now i feel like a rat.
i cant process this mans order because i forgot
to get his name and address. so ive decided to
mail every one of hayes bros. customers on the
computer joe left plugged in.
thats why youve got a copy of this letter. was it
you who talked to me last night. if so, please
write back c/o hayes bros. ltd. and let me know.
its a big order for joe and harry and i wouldnt
like to lose it.
also im sure you need your stuff. you certainly
sounded very anxious about that brief case.

yours sincerely,

s. mouse
hayes bros. ltd.

dear customer,

this is s. mouse of hayes bros. ltd. and im in
bigger trouble than i thought.
a man called up and said, whos this squeaking and
i said, s. mouse of hayes bros. ltd. and he said,
where do you get off, writing to people all over
the country and telling them my business.
i said, what do you mean and he said, i didn't
want anybody to know about the brief case.
why not, i said.
because i want it for my partner, he said.
as a birthday present, i said, and he said,
something like that.
so you want to keep it secret, i said and he gave
a funny laugh and said, yeah, secret, thats it,
secret.
i said, sorry.
he said, thats ok, just send the stuff out pronto
and dont mail any more letters telling people my
business.
yes, sir, i said. pronto, i said.
only in all the excitement i forgot to get his
name and address again.
thats why im writing a second time. even if it
wasnt you who talked to me last night, maybe it
was somebody you know, like your father or your

brother or your uncle.
id like you to ask around. if you find out who it
was who called, ring me at hayes bros. any night.
preferably soon.

yours sincerely,

s. mouse
hayes bros. ltd.

p.s. if it was you i talked to, please note i am
saying no more about the brief case you want for
your partner. i know how to keep a secret.

hayes bros. ltd. OFFICE SUPPLIES

8 Grafton Street, London W1X 3LA England   Tel: 0171 123 4789   Fax: 031 4933061

Directors: J. Hayes H. Hayes

dear customer,

this is s. mouse of hayes bros. ltd. and the
reason i dont use capital letters is i got short
legs.

last night, this guy rang and said, to whom am i
speaking and i said, to s. mouse of hayes bros.
ltd., thats whom.
he said, how come you dont use capital letters in
your letters, they look terrible.
i said, listen, buddy, its no fun standing on a
shift key trying to reach the other keys when you
have legs as short as mine.
he said, i never thought of that. he wasnt the
man who ordered the brief case though. i still
dont know who that was.

but i thought i better let you know about the
capital letters in case you were wondering too.

yours sincerely,

s. mouse
hayes bros. ltd.

hayes bros. ltd. OFFICE SUPPLIES

8 Grafton Street, London W1X 3LA England   Tel: 0171 123 4789   Fax: 031 4933061

Directors: J. Hayes H. Hayes

dear customer,

last night i found a fat envelope in the hayes
bros. post rack addressed personal to s. mouse of
hayes bros. ltd.
so i gnawed it open and inside was 5 thousand
pounds in used 5 pound notes and a handwritten
letter.

the letter said

This is to keep your mouth shut about
the brief case.
Have you sent it out yet? My partner
is due back from Bristol on Monday
so it is getting urgent.
The other stuff doesn't matter –
I only asked for it so the brief case
wouldn't look suspicious.
Just send it out and don't tell Harry
or Joe Hayes.
Or anybody.

P.S. Just make sure it's big enough to
hold half a million cash. Also, I
expect you to move fast.

the letter was not signed and there was no return
address.
have you asked your father and your brother and
your uncle yet. maybe you should ask around your
cousins too.
thank you.

yours sincerely,

s. mouse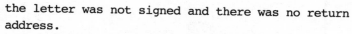
hayes bros. ltd.

p.s. im rich. im rich.

hayes bros. ltd. OFFICE SUPPLIES

8 Grafton Street, London W1X 3LA England   Tel: 0171 123 4789   Fax: 031 4933061

Directors: J. Hayes H. Hayes

DEAR CUSTOMER,

THIS IS S. MOUSE OF HAYES BROS. LTD. AND I HAVE
FOUND THE CAPS LOCK KEY.
THE CAPS LOCK KEY IS RIGHT DOWN ON THE BOTTOM
LEFT OF THIS COMPUTERS KEYBOARD WHICH IS WHY I
DIDNT NOTICE IT BEFORE.
IF YOU JUMP ON THE CAPS LOCK KEY IT STAYS DOWN,
NOT LIKE THE OTHER KEYS WHICH COME UP AGAIN.
WITH THE CAPS LOCK KEY DOWN EVERYTHING PRINTS OUT
IN CAPS.

I STILL CANT DO BRACKETS OR QUOTE MARKS OR THE
QUESTION MARK OR ANYTHING LIKE THAT, BUT I
BELIEVE MY LETTERS WILL LOOK BETTER ALL IN CAPS.
WHAT DO YOU THINK.

NOBODY RANG LAST NIGHT. IT WAS VERY PEACEFUL.

YOURS SINCERELY,

S. MOUSE
HAYES BROS. LTD.

DEAR CUSTOMER,

THIS IS S. MOUSE OF HAYES BROS. LTD. AND MY
FRIEND COCKROACH HAS GOT ME WORRIED.

COCKROACH DROPS IN TO SEE ME SOMETIMES AFTER JOE
AND HARRY GO HOME.

LAST NIGHT SHE SAID, YOU SHOULD BE CAREFUL ABOUT
SENDING OUT ANY BRIEF CASE BIG ENOUGH TO HOLD
HALF A MILLION SOVS.

WHAT ARE SOVS, I SAID.

POUNDS, DONT YOU KNOW ANYTHING.

I DONT KNOW SOVS, I SAID. WHY SHOULD I BE CAREFUL
ABOUT SENDING OUT THE BRIEF CASE.

SHE SAID, BECAUSE IT SOUNDS VERY SUSPICIOUS TO
ME. I SAID WHY. SHE SAID, THERE WAS A ROBBERY IN
BRISTOL ON TUESDAY.

THATS WHERE THIS MANS PARTNER IS COMING BACK
FROM, I SAID. COCKROACH SAID, I KNOW.

I SAID, HOW MUCH WAS TAKEN IN THE ROBBERY IN
BRISTOL AND SHE SAID, HALF A MILLION POUNDS.

I SAID, OH.

hayes bros. ltd. OFFICE SUPPLIES

8 Grafton Street, London W1X 3LA England   Tel: 0171 123 4789   Fax: 031 4933061

Directors: J. Hayes H. Hayes

DEAR CUSTOMER,

THIS IS S. MOUSE OF HAYES BROS. LTD. AND MY
FRIEND COCKROACH HAS GOT ME WORRIED.
COCKROACH DROPS IN TO SEE ME SOMETIMES AFTER JOE
AND HARRY GO HOME.
LAST NIGHT SHE SAID, YOU SHOULD BE CAREFUL ABOUT
SENDING OUT ANY BRIEF CASE BIG ENOUGH TO HOLD
HALF A MILLION SOVS.
WHAT ARE SOVS, I SAID.
POUNDS, DONT YOU KNOW ANYTHING.
I DONT KNOW SOVS, I SAID. WHY SHOULD I BE CAREFUL
ABOUT SENDING OUT THE BRIEF CASE.
SHE SAID, BECAUSE IT SOUNDS VERY SUSPICIOUS TO
ME. I SAID WHY. SHE SAID, THERE WAS A ROBBERY IN
BRISTOL ON TUESDAY.
THATS WHERE THIS MANS PARTNER IS COMING BACK
FROM, I SAID. COCKROACH SAID, I KNOW.
I SAID, HOW MUCH WAS TAKEN IN THE ROBBERY IN
BRISTOL AND SHE SAID, HALF A MILLION POUNDS.
I SAID, OH.

NOW IM CONFUSED. COCKROACH SAID I SHOULD PHONE
THE POLICE, BUT I DIDNT BECAUSE HARRY HAS BEEN
GIVING OUT TO JOE ABOUT THE SIZE OF THE PHONE
BILL.
BESIDES, IF I TELL THE POLICE ABOUT THE BRIEF
CASE THEY WOULD JUST LAUGH AT ME BECAUSE I DONT
KNOW THE MANS NAME AND ADDRESS.
THEY MIGHT ALSO WANT TO KNOW ABOUT THE 5 THOUSAND
POUNDS IN USED 5 POUND NOTES.
DO YOU THINK THE MAN WHO WANTS THE BRIEF CASE HAS
ANYTHING TO DO WITH THE ROBBERY IN BRISTOL.
AND WHAT SHOULD I DO IF HE PHONES AGAIN.
I WOULD VERY MUCH LIKE TO HAVE YOUR OPINION ON
THESE MATTERS.

YOURS SINCERELY,

S. MOUSE
HAYES BROS. LTD.

P.S. COCKROACH ISNT REALLY A COCKROACH, THATS
JUST HER NICKNAME. SHES A SPIDER.

dear customer,

this is s. mouse of hayes bros. ltd. and i have
broken the caps lock key.
i jumped up and down on it too hard and it broke.

cockroach says they dont make them like they used
to, but i think it broke because i got too
excited.
the man rang again last night and said, listen,
are you trying to mouse me up. you mean louse
you up, i said and he said, no, i mean mouse me
up. no, sir, i said, im not trying to mouse
anybody up.
he said, i suppose youll try to tell me you didnt
get the money i sent.
no, sir, i said, i wouldnt try to tell you that
at all.

then wheres my brief case, he said.
so i told him there was a problem. we are right
out of stock of brief cases, i said, but he didnt
believe me.
he said if he didnt get his brief case before
thursday he would put out a contract on me with a
hit cat.
then he hung up.
i still didnt get his name and address.
its been one of those nights.
cockroach said i should send him back the 5
thousand pounds. how can i, i said, when i dont
know his name and address. you are a plonker, i
said.
cockroach looked squashed.
if you hear anything at all about the robbery in
bristol, please phone me.

yours sincerely,

s. mouse
hayes bros. ltd.

p.s. actually, we arent out of stock on brief
cases at all. i only told him that. if you were
going to buy a brief case from hayes bros. ltd.,
i wouldnt want to mislead you.

p.p.s. maybe cockroach is right about the police.
getting laughed at is better than getting eaten
by a hit cat. ill sleep on it and maybe ring them
up tomorrow night.

dear customer,

this is s. mouse of hayes bros. ltd. and i would
appreciate it if you would consider doing me a
favour.
last night a woman phoned and said, is that
s. mouse and i said, yes, maam, this is s. mouse
of hayes bros. ltd. and she said, are you for real.
im for hayes bros. ltd., i said.
no, she said, i mean are you a real live mouse or
are you just some sort of publicity stunt.
then, before i could answer her, she said, i
mean, i keep getting these crazy letters from a
mouse and at first i thought they were just
written by some bozo trying to sell me office
supplies but now im not so sure so i decided to
phone up and find out for myself and here i am
actually talking to a mouse, for heavens sake.
and you certainly do talk a lot, i thought, but i
didnt say that. what i said was, maam, i am a
real mouse, i am not some bozo trying to sell you
office supplies.

then how come you can talk and type and do stuff
that other mice cant, she said.

i took a course in business administration, i
said.

then after that a man rang up and said, is that
s. mouse of hayes bros. ltd. yuk, yuk, yuk.

i said, this is he.

the man said, how would you like to come and work
for me, mouse, or may i call you s. yuk, yuk,
yuk.

no thank you, sir, i said. i am very happy
working here at hayes bros. ltd.

you could make a lot of money working for me,
yuk, yuk, yuk, he said.

i already have an elegant sufficiency, i said,
thinking about the 5 thousand pounds in the fat
envelope.

you slay me, mouse, you really do, the man said.

i wish i could, i said, but he didnt hear me.

these calls took up so much of my time i didnt
get to ring the police.
as a favour, could you not call me up to ask if
im for real or go yuk, yuk, yuk down the phone.
but do ring if you hear anything about the
robbery in bristol or the guy who wants the brief
case.

or if you want to buy any office supplies, of
course.

yours sincerely,

s. mouse 🐾
hayes bros. ltd.

hayes bros. ltd. OFFICE SUPPLIES

8 Grafton Street, London W1X 3LA England   Tel: 0171 123 4789   Fax: 031 4933061

Directors: J. Hayes H. Hayes

dear customer,

this is s. mouse of hayes bros. ltd. and my
friend cockroach told me british telecom dont
charge if you make a 999 call.
that finally persuaded me to ring the police.

old bill here, the policeman said.

hello, bill, i said, this is s. mouse of hayes
bros. ltd., and i want to report a robbery of
half a million pounds.

was that the one in bristol, he said.

yes, sir, i said. i have this man who wants me to
send him out a brief case and i think he plans to
use it to smuggle out the money.

do you have this mans name and address, bill
asked me.

no, sir, i admitted, i forgot to get it. i waited
for him to laugh at me, but he didnt.

is he likely to phone you again, he asked.
its possible, i said.

maybe we could put a tap on your phone, he said.
do you think harry hayes and joe hayes would
agree.
they might, i said, they use a lot of water to
make coffee.
actually i didnt think harry and joe would agree
to messing up their phone at all, but i didn't
want to argue since old bill was so nice.
one good thing though, he promised to send a
squad car round each night to keep an eye out for
the hit cat.

i am writing so you will realize our police are
wonderful.

yours sincerely,

s. mouse
hayes bros. ltd.

hayes bros. ltd. OFFICE SUPPLIES

8 Grafton Street, London W1X 3LA England Tel: 0171 123 4789 Fax: 031 4933061

Directors: J. Hayes H. Hayes

dear customer,

this is s. mouse of hayes bros. ltd. and that
noise inside joe hayes office is the cat.

he got in through the skylight while the
policemen in the patrol car were on their tea
break.

i should have known he might try something like
that since he was a professional.
fortunately joe hayes always locks his office
door when he goes home for the night, so the hit
cat cant get at me.

i was expecting him, of course, this being well
past thursday and i still havent been able to
send out the brief case.
when i heard him coming in, i made sure joes door
was locked. then i stuck my head through the
mousehole in the skirting and hurled abuse at
him.

he didnt like that.

when he found he couldnt get at me, he tried to
go back out onto the roof, but my friend
cockroach had closed the skylight.
so now hes trapped. and hes going to be in big
trouble when joe hayes comes in tomorrow because
i know for a fact joe is allergic to cats.

i guess that puts paid to one threat to my life.
i knew you would want to know.

yours sincerely,

s. mouse
hayes bros. ltd.

dear customer,

this is s. mouse of hayes bros. ltd. and im still
shaking like a leaf.

last night the man called about the brief case,
but not on the phone.
he rang the doorbell sometime after midnight and
when i wouldnt open up, he let himself in with a
credit card.
where are you, s. mouse, he shouted. i am going to
stomp you for what you done to my hit cat.
that wasnt me, i thought, that was joe hayes, but
i didnt want to argue since he was so big.
where are you, he called out again, where are you,
where are you.
i was inside the computer examining the circuitry,
but i didnt tell him. he opened up the filing
cabinet and all the desk drawers and he turned out
the waste-basket, all the time shouting, where are
you, s. mouse, where are you.

he looked behind the radiator and pulled some
books down off the shelves. he even looked inside
harry hayes liquor cabinet even though i am
teetotal.

then he quietened down a little and got this
funny look on his face and came over to the
computer.

i thought he was on to me but he just sat down
and switched on the computer and typed a
message.

i have merged his message with this letter so
you can read what he wrote.

You can't hide for ever, S. Mouse. You
think you are smart just because you
took my five grand and didn't send the
case. Well, let me tell you, nobody puts
one over on me. I have trapped better
mice than you. I'll be back after my
partner and I stash the money and when I
do, you'd better look out. You'll wish
you had never been born, S. Mouse. What
does the "S" in your name stand for
anyway? I bet it stands for SCUMBAG!

it was an abusive letter, but very well typed.
when he was done, he put down a piece of cheese,
stole a brief case and left.

i am writing so you will know what i am up
against.

also, will you keep your eyes open for a big
abusive man carrying a brief case that looks as
if it might contain half a million pounds.
if you see him, dont wait to ring me, call the
police and ask for my friend old bill.
tell him s. mouse of hayes bros. ltd. said you
were to call.

im sure he will remember me.

yours sincerely,

s. mouse
hayes bros. ltd.

p.s. my fur is no longer standing up on end and
the ringing in my ears has stopped. all the same,
it is no fun being inside a computer when
somebody switches on and writes a letter.
p.p.s. i ignored the cheese. im not stupid.

hayes bros. ltd. OFFICE SUPPLIES

8 Grafton Street, London W1X 3LA England   Tel: 0171 123 4789   Fax: 031 4933061

Directors: J. Hayes H. Hayes

dear customer,

this is s. mouse of hayes bros. ltd.
last night my friend cockroach called from
heathrow airport and told me the crooks were on
a plane to south america.
i said, are you all right, cockroach, and she
said, sure, it was a bit hot inside that brief
case but otherwise im fine.
i said, stick around and watch the fun. then
i called old bill.

i said, this is s. mouse of hayes bros. ltd. and
the guys who did the bristol robbery are just
about to board a plane for south america.

how do you know, he said.

i had them bugged, i said.

well get some squad cars round, he said.
just make sure theyre not on their tea break,
i said.
but old bill didnt hang about. his men snatched
the robbers right out on the tarmac.

all the money was in a hayes bros. brief case one
of them was carrying, except for 5 thousand
pounds which the police said had mysteriously

disappeared. cockroach got a lift back in the
squad car.

you may have read about it in the papers. mouse
makes mincemeat of robbers escape plan.

yours sincerely,

s. mouse
hayes bros. ltd.

MOUSE MAKES MINCEMEAT OF ROBBERS' ESCAPE PLAN

The massive £500,000 bank robbery in Bristol has now been solved ... by a mouse.

Timely action by S. Mouse of Hayes Bros. Ltd., a London office supply company, and his arachnid partner Cockroach, led to the apprehension of the robbers only minutes before they were set to make their escape to South America.

Mr Mouse told our reporters he became suspicious when one of the robbers ordered a brief case from Hayes Bros. Ltd. of the exact size needed to hold the money stolen in the robbery.

On Mouse's instructions, his colleague Cockroach hid in the brief case and alerted Mouse by phone from Heathrow

Airport when she discovered the robbers were about to leave the country. Mouse then called the police.

Plain-clothes detectives and uniformed patrolmen rushed to the airport and managed to apprehend the criminals as they were boarding the plane.

"They were armed and dangerous," said Inspector Katchum of the Yard. "If it hadn't been for the tip-off from the mouse, they would almost certainly have gotten clean away."

There is speculation that both S. Mouse and Cockroach are in line for Duke of Edinburgh Awards for bravery and may even be recommended for the New Year's Honours list.

hayes bros. ltd. OFFICE SUPPLIES

8 Grafton Street, London W1X 3LA England   Tel: 0171 123 4789   Fax: 031 4933061

Directors: J. Hayes H. Hayes

dear customer

this is s. hayes of mouse bros. ltd. and ive been
celebrating. ive stopped being teetotal this one
time because harry and joe read all about me in
the paper.

they were so pleased about the free publicity for
hayes bros. ltd. that they gave me a promotion.
also a substantial raise.

im very glad the way things have turned out.

yours sincerely,

s. mouse
night manager
hayes bros. ltd.

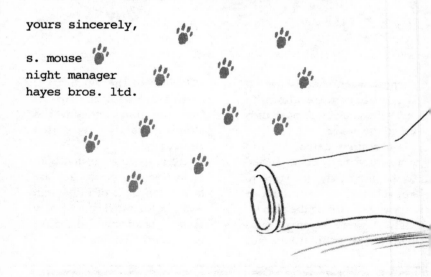

THE STONE THAT GREW
Enid Richemont

Katie finds the stone in an old box in the loft. It doesn't look like much at first, but then it does something amazing: it grows! Katie thinks it's wonderful. What's more, it's hers and she's not going to share it; it's bad enough having to share Mum with her little stepbrother, Jake. It might even be a way of getting in with Sarah and her gang. Meanwhile the stone continues to grow ... and grow!

MORE WALKER PAPERBACKS
For You to Enjoy